IMMORTAL SOUL

THE STORY

This book is a work of fiction.

IMMORTAL SOUL

THE STORY

Huni Hunfjord

Copyright © 2019 by Huni Hunfjord.

For information contact:

Kirkjuvegur 28, 230 Keflavik, Iceland

Phone: +354 821 1977

http://www.HuniHunfjord.com

Cover design by Huni Hunfjord and Image by Deflyne Coppens from Pixabay

Book design, editing and formatting by Huni Hunfjord

ISBN: 978-9935-9472-1-5

First Edition: September 2019

Here is a part of my story. I am amongst you. You might have passed me in the streets not knowing where I came from or where I am going. I totally understand that. What if, I would tell you right now, that I have been here for a very long time. Would you believe me? Well let's find out. This is my story.

A long, long time ago:
I can't see anything here. I am here in complete darkness. Even though I can't see anything right now, at the same time, I feel, what I can probably never properly explain to you mortal. I see nothing, yet at the same time I feel everything. Everything feels like you would probably compare to being deeply in love on earth, but that does not even come close to describing what I am feeling right here, in this space of emptiness and oneness at the same time. I feel like I am at home, but yet nothing makes sense to me right now.

I try to focus on my senses one by one. I

can't see anything, I can't smell anything and I certainly can't hear or taste anything here either. Where am I? I am not panicking, because I feel like I am back home, at the same time I don't sense anything around me here. I try to feel my body and I can feel it, but in a different way than I am used to. Right now it's more like a projection of a body.

Now after calming myself down even more, I start to expect to see what I need to see. I am going back to what has served me so well before. I am going to trust my intuition. This is more of a feeling than a thought. A dim light appears in front of me. As it gets brighter I start to see that I am in a room, or at least inside something that reminds me of a room. This feels like an artificial created room or a projection of a room. Yet it feels incredibly warm, even though it looks completely white. It's like the white color is hot and warm but still more brilliantly white than the brightest light you can see on earth. I told you I would probably have a hard time to explain this to you mortal soul, just bare with me as I take you on this journey with me and I promise to try my best to explain everything to you.

As the light becomes brighter, I sit here in the corner noticing that 13 other personalities or should I say entities are in the room with me now. Not all of them have a body they project, yet I understand that each entity has its own soul. They are all different personalities. I stand up and walk towards the group of entities in the room. Some of these 13 entities are simply light and others project a body. I think they are only doing that for me, to show me something I can relate to. I ask the entity, where am I? The leading entity tells me that this is a place where I review my life. What, am I dead, I ask. What you think is death, is really more like awakening, the entity explains to me. What do you mean, am I now finally awake? The entity replies, yes you are finally awake now. After many lifetimes you are finally awake. Wait, hold up a minute, many lifetimes, and never been awake before, what does all this really mean? You are now fully conscious in this dimension for the first time now between lives. Other times you have experienced this part as you would probably refer to as a dream. Then you spent your time in a dense physical environment created by your expectations and imagination. This is the reason why there are so many tales told of what the afterlife looks like. It's based on the persons perspective until the soul finally awakens in this dimension. You keep being reincarnated until you awaken, then you can be effectively guided towards your destination.

I ask them who they are and what they represent. I get the reply that these are the 13 volunteers that have been guiding me. I ask the entity what I should call it and it replies, you can call me Fritz. I just realized that I have not been talking with these entities verbally, but I have been telepathically communicating with them. In this form I have also become genderless. Each soul becomes genderless in a place like this. But I do have strong memories of my past life and relate to myself right now as male, knowing I am neither or both. I start to ask questions about my existence and I am getting priceless answers, and questions thrown back at me. To make this easier for you mortal soul to read, we will not get to deep into the meaning of life and all that, for now anyway.

I start to move, walk or glide towards Fritz, whatever you would call it, because right now I do not have a body like you understand what a body is. Once I reach Fritz, I ask him what he represents. He tells me that he is the one communicating on behalf of the 13 spirit guides that volunteered to guide me through my lifetimes. He explains that all souls have spirit guides that volunteer to guide a soul on it's journey of growth and learning. Sometimes these spirit groups add on new guides and sometimes some leave the group when they are not needed anymore. Or like in my case, I have had the same core 13 spirit guides for a very long time now. He further explains that they can call on any expert guides when needed for some specific tasks or experiences that need more specific guidance.

This is the place where we all visit to review what we have learned once we awaken on our journey. This is the place between lives. I can't believe it, but at the same time I know it's true! I start talking with Fritz about what I remember from my last past life experience.

This life was lived on a planet far away from earth and I was what you mortal soul would call an alien during this lifetime, but for me I was just Z, an inhabitant of the planet Arcturus. I remember my mission as a grown adult where I flew my spaceship to this strange planet that used to possess life. As I was looking down from my aircraft to a planet that looked like it had chrome colored ground, or maybe what you would consider something like Mars, but this was definitely not Mars. I looked through the fog of the clouds covering the planet, knowing that I was there on a research mission to see what had happened to this planet. I started to see through the fog, the bones on the red deserted ground and they looked like human remains, or similar. I saw that there was no vegetation or any plants growing there. It looked like this planet had already died. I can see my body as I am remembering this lifetime. As I was controlling the aircraft, I see that I had four fingers on each hand and they look bluish. I can feel my slim body as I reminisce this past life of mine. I feel that my skull is much bigger and longer than what you might consider a normal skull on earth. My mission was all about taking samples from this dead planet and studying why it died. Once I collected the samples of this hot rock we used to call a planet, I returned to my own planet Arcturus. My mission was complete and once I returned to my home, I was back with my family.

The houses on my planet looked like something you might compare to a tree house, but we don't build them in trees. We make them out of a material not known to your world on earth. You might compare it to titanium but the material is much better for construction than titanium. It's much more moldable and more durable. I realize this might seem strange to you, but this is the truth. I lived on the 24th floor of our branch bubble house with my family. I had a wife, five children and three grandchildren. On Arcturus the children know what their mission in life is before they reach puberty, at the age of 10 years old. Which is really like 35 years old compared to planet earth's time.

Now I can recall one of the most important time in this life. It is when we have served our purpose and we are ready to depart. Each Arcturian knows before his life is about to expire and the family gathers around the individual to say their goodbyes. We have a big party knowing that we are taking the next step in our journey to advance as souls in the cosmic universe. On earth we mourn the deceased, but on Arcturus we celebrate the departure of a loved one and feel the deep love and joy as they pass on to the next level of their soul's journey.

Fritz now asks me what I have learned from this past life lived?
I told him my lesson from this life was acceptance, love and being happy with the life path chosen.

Fritz asks if I am ready to go onto the next phase of my soul's journey. I reply that I am more than ready, not knowing what will happen next.

Now you have an opportunity to be born on earth, he says. Are you ready to experience the duality of life? Yes I am, I proclaim. Are you sure?

You know that all you knowledge you have gathered during your previous lives must be forgotten when you get there. I am ready, I said with pride and love. You know you will be born as a helpless baby in this world without memories of your spiritual growth. Are you sure you are ready? I say that I am ready, as this is something many of us have wanted to volunteer for. To be born an earthling.

I felt tremendous pressure as I was being brought into this world of duality. Yes, I remember it like it's happening right now. I was born as the son of a pharaoh in Egypt. My childhood was splendid and I had everything I ever wanted and needed. I was well liked and I had a beautiful body as I grew into my adulthood. As I grew into a man, I had to have sex with many women, but that is not what I really wanted. I was eager to learn how to be a good pharaoh. I was trained to use a whip at an early age and into my teen years. I was learning how to whip and discipline the slaves we had. I didn't want to do that, but I did it because it was expected of me.

When I was about to take my place as the new pharaoh, my sexual urges had taken over and I had a male lover by then. It was one of our chamber servants. This was not acceptable in our kingdom, so I kept it a secret. I kept sleeping with women, but my love was for this boy called Jabare which means "a man known for his bravery". We were sneaking off to the side to indulge in our pleasures when we could, but I was expected to have sex with the ladies until I would be suited with a bride to be. This became harder and harder as time passed. I just wanted to be who I am! I just wanted to be lovable and love all of my people, not to be with women or hurt anyone either.

One night as I and my lover were making passionate love, I could hear the chambermaids whispering about this encounter. I knew this could possibly ruin my life path, so I told the guards to round up all the chambermaids. I did not realize that one of the guards had already told the pharaoh's most trusted general what had happened. I went to sleep that night alone and as the moon hovered above the sphinx, I was murdered in my bed. I know in my heart that it was my father that gave the final command, but he would never admit to that.

I know this place! I am back in the warm white room now fully conscious, as I remember my past life lived on earth. Where are you Fritz, I ask. The lights come slowly on and he and the other 12 spirit guides are surrounding me now. Well, what did you learn, Fritz asks me, with a humorous tone. Yes, that's right, even entities like spirit guides have a sense of humor.

Fritz has lived a life of an incarnation, but not all spirit guides have done so. This makes Fritz more relatable and probably why he was chosen to present the group as I advance on my soul's journey.

I tell them that I learned that you should never ever look down on anyone. We are all light beings experiencing what we need to evolve to the next soul's level. Be who you are and it's OK. Be true to yourself, love life, love yourself as you are and love everyone at the same level as yourself.

Very interesting, Fritz replies. All of the sudden I remember all my past lives all at once and I now realize how much I still have to learn and experience. I ask Fritz, if I am ready for my next reincarnation?

Before I hear the answer, I found myself in the body of a young girl in the jungle. I was all alone and no one around me. I was picked up by this tribe called Kaixana, who took me into their tribe. Even though they cared for me, I felt like an outsider in the tribe my whole life. I was always fascinated by nature and the power the old shaman in the village had, or at least the power that he seemed to have. I studied him from afar and watched him as much as I could. I would often run into the forest and try finding the same roots and leaves he was using in his remedies. I would try to make my own cocktails without letting anyone know where I was or what I was doing. I soon started to practice with my own medicine on injured animals, plants and trees.

One day, I was in the jungle, when the shaman found me practicing and imitating his practices there. This could have been my last day in that lifetime, but instead he decided to teach me in secret. He said I had great potential to become a great shaman myself, but the tribe would not accept this. At least not right away. For the next few years I would practice to become a shaman. He taught me how to connect with trees through my energy points in my body, which are also called chakras. He was always guiding me. I became more and more connected to nature and felt my divine guidance, but not realizing that I knew all of my 13 personal spirit guides already. The shaman helped me build a house in the jungle that I started to stay more and more in by myself. One day the shaman brought a young girl to my hut. She had severe fever and was in and out of consciousness. He told me to make her a brew from a specific root that only grows around the river bed. I stayed with this very sick girl for three days without sleeping. I would rub the mixture I made from the roots on her chest and give her one drop on her tongue each time she regained consciousness. At the end of the three days, she fully recovered.

It was time to tell the tribe what I had become. I was invited to the ceremony were the shaman bestowed me the title of a shaman. From that day forward, the whole tribe would always come to see me if there was anything that needed attention, in regards to health and food related subjects. I slowly became respected for my gifts, but I never moved back into the tribe again. I spend all my time in the jungle, in the house that my master shaman and I built together many years ago. I was getting better and better at receiving messages from my guides and connecting with the spirit of the jungle, the elementals. Until the last day in that lifetime, I kept learning new things about nature and the flow of life and most importantly, I was happy. Once my time had come, I remember cooking a meal earlier that day, in my cooking pot, in my hut. I had bean stew, my favorite food to eat. I remember eating the bean stew with my fingers as I felt my time had come. I cleaned up after the meal and laid down in my sleeping area and closed my eyes.

I am home again. I glide towards my 13 spirit guides in the warm white room. Not bad, Fritz says. I start to laugh. Yes, that was a very interesting and rewarding experience. So, what did you learn this time, Fritz asks me. I learned that being alone can be a very rewarding experience and that not being dependent on anyone else is OK. I am enough!

Very good, Fritz says, and adds that now they want to invite me to go into a soul group meeting. Because my next reincarnation is going to be at a very historical point in time and you will be remembered for a long time in the history books on earth. He tells me that I play a part in a narrative, but at the same time I need to remember that even though many things are known, even more events are not written in stone, so to speak. This is all a blueprint with possibilities. Look at your path as a highway and if you live your life according to your own plan, then you travel on the highway, but with free will you can always turn off the highway. During this soul group meeting we will discuss all these possibilities, are you ready? I am.

I feel my essence being brought into a big hall. As I enter the great hall, I form into the body from my past life lived. I can clearly feel and see my body now. It seems like it's no longer a projection, but something more like you experience on earth, yet a bit different. I am standing here looking at many other people in this great hall. I know them all. Fritz says that this is my soul group and that they take on their last body lived, in the great hall, as it makes it easier to converse about the past and the possible future we are about to embark on.

Since this place has no time, I cannot tell you how long it took, but if I would make an earthly guess, I would guess it was a few years that we spent going over our paths chosen and how each soul could get what they needed to evolve in this next big adventure. We went over every possible scenario, when we take the off ramp of the chosen highway and how it impacts the other souls and how they can then have other opportunities to learn their lessons. The further we get into our planning the less visible our bodies become. Now I am brought back into the white warm room with my personal spirit guides, which are sometimes also known as, thought adjusters. Fritz says, now it's time to be born at a historical event in time, remember to enjoy the experience! There is no right or wrong, it's all just a learning experience, he adds.

I was raised in the great city of Rome. I loved to go into the square as a young boy and watch the beggars and the sick. I would sit on one of the rooftops and watch them as often as I could. When I turned 14, I was taken away to train with the army. This was during the first year of our new emperor Tiberius. Next few years I was trained and then trained some more. I got to see the world, but not exactly as I had envisioned. I witnessed a lot of murders and brutality as I served my emperor. I was scared of my emperor like so many of my fellow soldiers. I had a wife by then, but had only spent about 2 years with my wife, as I was always on the road making war or enforcing some strange laws to keep us all separated in classes. Classes of the poor, middle and rich. Then the priests were put into a totally different class of their own.

I always read when I could, and I loved learning about the world. I had started to hear rumors about this king that had been born about the same time I was born. This was supposedly the messiah. I started to hear more and more about this man, that was preaching love and compassion amongst people. I was fascinated and so were a few of us in the Roman army. We kept this fascination a secret of course, as this was something that could have severe consequences for us and our families. I hoped this was the man that would free me and my wife from my duties, which I experienced as slavery. Even though many looked at this slavery as a great honor, I did not. I started to hear about this man's sermons and that he had now about 12 disciples that were often seen with him and around him when he spoke to people. I also started to hear the other side of this growing problem for the Roman empire.

It seemed inevitable at that time, that Tiberius wanted this mad man gone, because too many people were starting to follow him. By chance, one day, I heard three Roman soldiers talking about Jesus. I wanted to know what they were plotting. Did they want to go and follow Jesus? I surely wanted that, because I knew in my heart that this was no ordinary man. I believed in Jesus, but at the same time, I never told anyone that.

I found out that these three soldiers were going to meet with one of Jesus's disciples. I wanted to join, knowing this might be life threatening if someone would find out. I looked down at my feet and saw my sandals making their way down a few stairs that lead into the basement of a two story house in a small town right outside of Jerusalem. Once I came into this room, there was not much light in there. Only one oil lamp in the far corner of the basement. A man walked into the room and introduced himself as Judas.

This conversation felt like an out of body experience for me. Almost like a dejavu. It was like I was looking down on the five of us there, talking about how we could help Jesus to step into his role of the messiah, who would free his people from tyranny. Judas paid us with 30 pieces of silver to create a scenario, were Jesus would have to show his godly power, take over and lead the people into a time of peace and love. We stayed in this basement for a few days, only leaving the basement to use the toilet. We used our time there to prepare this scenario methodically in details.

Once the day came to take action, we walked directly to the Garden of Gethsemane. As we entered the garden, we were met by other soldiers with a different agenda. The other three soldiers quickly aborted our mission and joined the other soldiers in arresting Jesus. Judas was already at the garden by this time with a baffled look on his face. He reeked of shame. Even though Judas had good intentions, he did not know that one of the three other soldiers had leaked out the information and therefore he betrayed Jesus, accidentally. I froze and watched this whole scenario in shock. I knew Jesus would be killed in custody. Later, the three soldiers changed their story as you might know it. They told everyone that they paid Judas 30 pieces of silver to betray Jesus, but that was not the truth. Judas did not betray Jesus on purpose, he did his very best to prevent the inevitable, I knew that. Jesus apparently knew this also, that Judas would betray him by his actions. Though Jesus spoke to Judas kindly, he greeted him as a traitor when he arrived at the garden.

I was one of the guards given the task to guard the crosses that day. Many people gathered around to watch their promised messiah hanging on the cross that day. The air was thick with grief and a lot of tears hit the soil that day. He had been tortured and he was bleeding. His hair was wet from sweat and blood. As I looked at this man suffering on the cross I felt great empathy. He raised his head up, as I looked at him and he looked straight into my eyes. I cannot describe the love and peace that came from this man's face. It was incredible and I knew what I should do. I knew this man understood me and my actions. Without thinking I quickly ran my spear into his side, right under his rib cage, to put him out of his misery. I did it as an act of mercy as I felt his pain, suffering on the cross that day. I did not think about the consequences, I just reacted. Moments later I felt something entering into my back. I was murdered.

As I thought I was about to go back to the white warm room, I was greeted by Jesus himself. I went to him and he smiled. I had no remorse, I only felt love and light. He said to me "Peace be upon you".

Fritz says to me, welcome back! I am filled with love and I feel the strength and love from all 13 of my spirit guides. What did you learn this time, Fritz asks me. I feel such love right now and my whole being is buzzing with euphoric ecstasy, as I reply that I have learned you can make mistakes. When you make mistakes with the intention of love and compassion, and you make them based on your best ability aiming for the highest good then there is no karma. In my heart I did what I thought was right and I realize that I will not be remembered as the man who ended Jesus's suffering, but something worse. I start laughing at this whole scenario, and so does Fritz.

After a short while, which could easily be a few earth years for all I know, Fritz says, now let's continue your soul's journey. Are you ready?

I was sitting on top of a mountain looking down on the clouds below. I was wearing striped clothes, something like pajamas. I didn't recognize these clothes that I was wearing and I certainly did not know where I was or how I got there. I was in a body of a healthy male about 30 years old, I would guess. My skin tone was a little dark, something like you would recognize in Asia. I felt very much out of place there. I stood up and walked towards chanting I heard behind me. I walked up four steps into a temple on the mountaintop. This temple had a classical Chinese structured roof. As I walked into the temple the chanting became louder. I saw an alter at the far end of the temple and four big columns on each side. Behind each column was a monk sitting in the lotus position and chanting. There was something burning on the altar, some statues and strange rocks there.

As I tried to talk with the monks, they said nothing. I was pointed to sit down beside the entrance. I was given an orange robe to put on and a bamboo mat to sit on. This was such an interesting experience to say the least. Who was I, and how did I get there?

The next few weeks went into learning their way of life. I remember trying to eat the rice with my fingers, but one of the monks hit my fingers as I tried to use my hands. He handed me strange sticks and displayed how I should eat my meal. I was sitting on the floor at a table with five other monks who did not speak a single word to me. During the next 20 years at the temple, I never heard them speak one word. The only sound they made was the chanting, which I was then a part of.

I was in my 50's heading down the mountain for the first time. Saying goodbye to my brothers, or in other words saying goodbye without using words. I was heading down the mountain to find out who I was, and how I got there. Even without words, I had learned some incredible deep truths about life, through their teachings. I traveled for a few weeks before I came to a bridge in a small town. I went to sit under an old bodhi tree by the bridge to meditate. As I fell into the field of endless possibilities, I was shown a vision 20 years ago.

As I was walking over the bridge, I was jumped by two men, who started to beat me up. They took everything I had on me. Then dumped me into the river, that runs under the bridge. I was unconscious but thankfully the thick grass sticking out of the water kept my body facing up. If not for the thick grass growing from the bank and into the river, I would have drowned that day. The next day, two monks found me unconscious in the river. That was the day I was taken up to the mountains.

As I came out of my meditation, I knew who I was and where I came from. I traveled for a few days until I came to the village I was from. I knocked on the door. A woman in her late 20's with dark hair came to the door. Oh my god, it was my niece. She recognized me. The next few years I was living back with my family and sharing my wisdom with those who wanted to listen. I was a writer before I lost my memory and I still had this keen ability to teach life lessons by telling stories that fascinated people. My stories were entertaining and full of wisdom for those who understood the lessons. I was sitting in a room with 5 children in front of me, with their eyes wide open, soaking in my stories. The grownups stood behind me, as eager as the children to hear new stories about life and the lessons life has to offer.

I became the wise old man in town. I would get up early each day and meditate. Then head into town and let life lead me forward to the people who wanted to listen to my stories and learn. I passed away at a very old age, embraced and loved by my family.

What did you learn this time, Fritz says. I do not need any words to learn to remember who I am or who I was. The answers all come from within, whatever it is that we want to remember or learn. I learned that humans can master their bodies and that we do not need much to thrive in life. Being a teacher is as important as it is to be a good student. Helping others to learn life lessons is something that greatly enriches your experience. Just being and teaching is greatly rewarding and it has nothing to do with worldly riches.

Very interesting, Fritz replies. He tells me that now I will get a chance to learn about cause and effect with this next incarnation. I am ready.

I was standing outside my home as a young boy living only with my father. We had traveled from afar to reach this promised land of opportunities. I found myself outside the house my father had built in this new land, looking at the trees surrounding our new home. I remember asking my father about my mother and he told me that she got sick and died on our journey to this new land of freedom. I went inside our home and sat down to eat my favorite meal with my father. We had meat and beans that day. Everything in our home was made from the woods around our home, except for a few personal items my father had brought with us. Like the silver framed painting of my father and mother together. They looked young and happy on that painting. My father always wore a hat, except when we sat down to eat together, then he would take the hat off. I was about 9 years old, wearing overalls that I had gotten from the nearest town, about four hours of riding distance from our house.

When my father rode off to find work, I would stay at home and wait for him. Sometimes it was days that he stayed on the road. I had a knife I loved and I would stay for days on the porch with my knife carving things out of wood. I kept getting better and better at carving figures out of wood and I would always greet my father with a gift I had carved for him when he finally came back home. All my figures got a special place on one of our shelves in the house. My father told me that these were his favorite most precious possessions he had. He said they represented my growth and love.

One day, I was sitting on the porch carving my next masterpiece and looking forward to giving it to my father when he would return. He never returned home from that trip. Next I found myself sitting inside a church looking at my father's coffin in the middle of the isle. I felt so little and helpless knowing that from now on it was only going to be me and no one else. I did not shed a tear, because I was afraid to show the other people in the church that I felt little and helpless. Maybe the people that killed my father were inside the church that day. How was I going to provide food for myself from now on?

I could not breathe as I felt my legs kicking in the air. A surge of adrenaline rushed through my body as I fought for my life that day. I took both hands and tried to grab onto the rope that was tied around my neck. A few seconds later I blacked out.

What did you learn this time around, Fritz asks me. I have no idea what this life lesson was all about, honestly. Maybe the lesson was that life is not always fair. I feel my energy in great imbalance right now and I don't know if I want to go again. Fritz looks at me with great empathy and love and says that now that I have lived a traumatized life and still seem to be energetically imbalanced from this experience, that it's time to go into a soul recovery session. I am guided to a place with lots of trees and a very beautiful picturesque scene. Here I get to converse with soul experts on my experience on the soul level. I learn that karma is nothing else than cause and effects. Once I realized that this life lived was also a part of my soul's growth and that this was experienced as an effect of taking another person's life in my previous lives lived, I become centered again. I realize the balance of cause and effects. I did not realize until now that karma can cross over many lifetimes.

I am now back with my 13 spirit guides ready to continue my soul's journey. Fritz comes closer to me and says that often it's the hardship and seemingly unfair experiences that grow the soul the most. I know this is true. My soul is in complete balance and I am ready for my next lesson now.

I found myself in a teenage body of a woman standing in a field, in front of a big lake. I was wearing a white beautiful dress. I looked down at my feet and saw that I was wearing beautiful white laced shoes that matched my dress. I felt healthy and fit. I lived in a wooden cabin with my parents and my grandfather. That day I sat down with my family to eat bean stew casserole. My mother brought the food from the fire stove placed in the middle of the cabin to the table. All the furniture was made from wood and we had a nice little porch outside. I loved sitting on the porch at night to watch the sun drop down behind the trees on the other side of the lake.

My family was very supportive of me and I got to be who I wanted to be. I was not interested in the boys because I was very preoccupied with my dream to become a teacher. I started to build a schoolhouse in my teens. After reaching my 20's I was teaching children in the small but wonderful school my father and grandfather had helped me build. I loved to teach. Children are so open to new ideas and each time I taught them at my school, I felt my inner light shine brightly.

A few years into my teacher role, I experienced my first true loss in life when I was walking behind the horse carriage with a wooden coffin on the back. We were taking my grandfather to the cemetery to be buried that day. As we traveled slowly through town I noticed how many people had gathered for my grandfather's funeral, all wearing their best attire for the occasion. He was well respected and I did not realize how many people knew him, until that day. I was very sad that my best friend had just passed away.

I kept on teaching the children at my school, even though I knew people were talking about this crazy lady, that had no idea what a woman's role in society should be. People looked at me as someone out of place. I realized that I was allowed to carry on with my work, because of the respect people had for my grandfather, but would they still stand idle by, after he was no longer around?

A few months later, I stood in front of my school burning to the ground. Someone obviously wanted to put me in my place. I became scared and I did not rebuild the school after the arson. But I did occasionally teach, but in secret.

I was in my 40's when I became pregnant. This was yet another thing for people to gossip about. Women should not be raising children at that age. I was too old to have a child, people kept telling me. I started to keep to myself, knowing that I would not get any support from anyone except my parents, that were still healthy at that time.

My water broke that day. My mother got some hot water and towels and sat with me. She told my father to wait outside while I brought this wonderful soul into this world. I felt the labor was a very difficult one, probably more than it should be, but of course I did not have anything to compare it to. Once the babies head was starting to come out, I felt something happening inside of me. As the baby came out, I felt light headed. I noticed that blood kept dripping on the ground as my mother held the crying baby in the slime and blood covered blanket she had wrapped around the baby. I felt my consciousness slowly fading as I kept losing a lot of blood. My mother handed me, my beautiful newborn baby. As I looked into the beautiful face of this innocent newborn soul, my vision became blurry. I felt so much love for this person. As I felt both my parents lay their hands on me, I felt the pain suddenly fade away.

Fritz greets me as I am back in the warm white room now. What did you learn this time around, Fritz asks me. Be yourself, your true self. Do what you are passionate about, even if it means swimming against the social stream of what is known as normal. Allow yourself to do what you love and let your inner light shine brightly on those who you can influence in a positive way. Remember the light that shines brightly within you, always. Use it as your compass. The brighter your light shines the more you are on the right path for your soul's growth.

Do you want to head back to the soul recovery now, after experiencing this trauma? I tell him that I feel balanced and that I am ready to continue.

I was raised on a farm in Kentucky. I was a typical young man that was drafted into the military after finishing high school. Just like my work ethics on the farm, I worked really hard on advancing my career in the US military. I advanced to the air force after a short time spent in the military. I had great skills as a pilot and I loved flying. I met my wife before world war 2. After having only spent a couple of years on the farm with my wife, I was called back in for duty. Me and my wife wanted to have children but she was not pregnant by the time I was shipped overseas to join the growing battle in Europe. I was stationed in the United Kingdom and flew with their air force for a few months. Most of our flights were recon flights, gathering information and taking pictures. But slowly this changed to start dropping bombs on high priority targets in Germany.

On May 28th 1944 I had my high priority

target. As I approach the target, my plane got hit by bullets. One of the bullets went through the body of the plane and through me as well. I was bleeding fiercely, but made the drop and managed to land the plane on neutral grounds barely conscious.

For the next nine days I was in a hospital unconscious. As I rose from my bed and looked down onto my own body. I realized that I was out of my body, but not dead, or at least not knowing if I was dead or not. I thought to myself that if I was dead, then why was I not in the warm white room by now? I was hovering above my body and I saw a silver cord connecting myself to the body laying there below me. A brief thought came to mind. I thought about my wife. As soon as this thought entered my mind, I was on the farm in Kentucky looking at my wife. She looked like she was doing OK. I saw her attending our garden. I stayed with her until she went to bed that night. On several occasions I tried to touch her and each time I did, she felt something. She could not hear me nor feel me, but yet she knew somehow that something was there with her. I saw her kissing our picture before she laid down for the night. After she fell asleep I thought about how I really wanted to know what was going on. As soon as that thought entered my mind, a man appeared in the room. He was in the same form I was, I saw his body, but it was like mine. More like pure energy formation of a body than physical form. He told me that I was needed at the soul council.

I had instantly been transported to a beach. I know this beach, I thought. It was the beach I had dreamed about in this lifetime. It was my magical beach I would go to in my mind when I needed timeout and when I thought about what my dream life would be like. It was always at this specific beach. A few entities sat by a fire on the beach waiting for me. They started to telepathically communicate with me. This is your chance to back out from you life path, they told me. I told them I did not understand. As soon as this question popped into my mind I knew the answer.

I sat down at a soul group meeting before this reincarnation and my plan involved bringing in two other souls in this lifetime from my soul group. I also knew that many of us get two exit ramps of the chosen highway path of life, where we can exit our life before our mission and lessons are complete. They explained that I would not be able to walk again in that lifetime, but I could finish this lifetime and complete my task of bringing in the two souls from my soul group, but also I could decide to exit now. I could enter quickly back into my soul group back on earth to complete my mission and lessons in another reincarnation. I told them I understood, but I was not ready to quit yet.

The next days I traveled all over the world looking at different things and people, seeing the world from another dimension. Each day I would go back to the hospital room and look at my lifeless body unconscious on the hospital bed. On June 6th 1944, I decided to redo my mission. This also became a very significant day in the war, known as D-day.

Fritz tells me that this is OK, we have these exit ramps on purpose and you have free will. Now we will get you right back into the game, he tells me. But before you go back, what did you learn in this lifetime, Fritz asks me. I learned about out of body experiences and that we can enter into other dimensions while still in physical form. I learned the truth about free will and learned that even though we do not complete our intended lessons we can get another chance to learn them. I am ready.

I found myself in the body of a young woman. I was wearing a red dress and shiny red high heels. I was wearing expensive jewelry that my husband had gotten me. I had not finish high school but felt that I was on a fast track to wealth by then. I was only 18 years old, married to a very wealthy older man. That day we sat down at the dinner table with his three children eating steak. I was what his friends called a trophy wife.

My husband decided to take me on a trip to the south east coast, in our new 1968 blue Chevrolet Bel Air Coupe. I felt the wind in my hair as I rolled down the window to smell the sea breeze. My husband told me to close the window and reached over to roll the window up as he was driving the car on a winding beach road. As he reached over me, to roll the window up, there was a turn coming up on the road ahead. I tried to tell him, but before I could, he pulled the steering wheel to the left a little bit too late and a little bit too hard. As the car slid sideways on the road, a truck slammed head on into our car, through the passenger door, where I was sitting.

Fritz is laughing. Well that was quick, he says. What did you learn this time? I learned what it is like to choose a life of comfort. I was not happy, I just appeared that way. Financial security means nothing for your soul's journey, if you are not following your dreams and purpose. I did not finish my soul group mission Fritz, what can I do to make up for that? Is there anything I can do and if so I am ready. You will have more spiritual guidance this time, now that you have a third chance to try to bring these two souls you planned to bring into this world of duality.

I was born again the year 1977 in Europe. I was always very independent and I remember as a young healthy boy to travel cross country to work on a farm in the summertime. I was very active and always asking questions about life. As I grew into a healthy teenager I felt the urge to move abroad. In the town I was raised in, it was greatly influenced by the US army stationed there and I saw the United States of America as the land I really wanted to move to, but how could I possibly do that?

Once I reach 17 years old I was playing basketball and tried to get into a high school in America. I was all set to go and join a family in Pennsylvania. A week before my departure, their oldest son got divorced and moved back home. That meant that the family could not accommodate me there anymore and it looked like I was not going to move to the states after all. At 20 years old a series of unfortunate events led to the death of a head basketball coach at a university in Kentucky. The newly hired coach had contacts in Europe that he reached out to, trying to find two basketball players he was willing to offer a full scholarship to, for playing basketball for the university in Kentucky. I was one of the basketball players offered a full scholarship in Kentucky. During my next 5 years in Kentucky I got married and I brought two souls into this existence in Kentucky.

The next few years I worked many different jobs after moving back to Europe after my divorce and graduating from the university. I lived in five different countries and remarried in 2007. I brought another baby into this world in 2011.

I was at a mental breaking point in 2012 when I moved back to the US, living in Florida at the time. At this low point in my life I was 35 years old and I was given a book to read. That was the day my spirit guides stepped into my life with unquestionable results. I read the book in a few days and saw the world like I had never done before. Before that day I thought I was dyslexic. Only to realize that the books I had tried to read before that time did simply not interest me enough to finish them. That was the year my spiritual journey while incarnated really took off. In 2015 I got divorced again and my spiritual journey was thrown into overdrive as I started to learn from accomplished entrepreneurs, healers and spiritual leaders around the world. The next few years I read everything I could get my hands on, on spirituality and prosperity. I was guided daily to dive deep into remembering who I am and who I was.

In 2018 I finally met my spirit guides in this physical form through hypnosis. I had my first lucid dream where I met my higher self and I had my first out of body experience traveling to other dimensions. By 2019 I had revisited many of my previous lifetimes lived and my bond with my 13 personal spirit guides was getting stronger by the day. This was the year that Fritz and the other 12 guides, guided me to write my story for you during this lifetime.

I am awake now. Are you?

This was a part of my story. I am amongst you right now. You might have passed me in the streets not knowing where I came from or where I am going, and that's OK.

LEARN MORE ABOUT THE AUTHOR, HUNI HUNFJORD

http://HuniHunfjord.com
http://IcyDesign.com
http://amazon.com/author/hunihunfjord

BOOKS BY HUNI HUNFJORD

Immortal Soul
You Are Freaking Awesome
The Mentorian
Our Road without Boundaries
Læringinn
Top 1% Parents Raise Top 1% Children
Sleeping Habits and Routines
Energy Flow
Manifest Meditation
Hugsköpun
Orkuflæði
Sub Talk - Deep Relaxation Subconscious
Talk - Volume 1, 2, 3, 4, 5 and 6